T H E

Tsunami

SADDLEBACK
EDUCATIONAL PUBLISHING

T H E   H E I G H T S

Blizzard	Ransom
Camp	River
Crash	Sail
Creature	Shelter
Dam	Score
Dive	Swamp
Heist	Treasure
Jump	**Tsunami**
Mudslide	Twister
Neptune	Wild

Original text by Ed Hansen
Adapted by Mary Kate Doman

SADDLEBACK
EDUCATIONAL PUBLISHING
www.sdlback.com

ISBN-13: 978-1-61651-673-4
ISBN-10: 1-61651-673-9
eBook: 978-1-61247-377-2

Printed in Malaysia

20 19 18 17 16   3 4 5 6 7

Chapter 1

Lilia sat by the window watching the snow fall. School was closed because of the storm. Lilia and her brothers spent two hours shoveling the driveway. The Heights was a great place, but winter was sometimes too cold!

Antonio was upstairs on his computer. And Franco was home from college doing laundry. Lilia went into the kitchen to talk to her parents.

"Hey, Lilia," said her dad, Rafael. "Get your brothers. I have some news."

When all five Silvas were in the kitchen, Rafael surprised them.

"Your mom and I just made vacation plans. I'm going to Australia tomorrow for work," said Rafael. "You guys will meet me there when my project is finished. We'll all fly to Vanuatu from there."

The three Silva kids looked at each other.

"Vanna who?" Lilia asked.

"V-a-n-u-a-t-u," Ana responded. "It's a group of islands in the South Pacific. It's a three-hour flight from Sydney, Australia."

"They are islands in a part of the South Pacific called Oceania," said Rafael. "Beautiful flowers and birds are everywhere. And there's great scuba diving. We can even hike up a live volcano."

"Awesome!" Antonio smiled. "I've always wanted to see a volcano. Sign me up."

"You're already signed up," Rafael laughed. "You'll be there in three weeks."

"Hey, Dad," said Franco. "Aren't those islands part of the Ring of Fire?"

"Say what?" exclaimed Lilia.

"It's a part of the world with a number of volcanos. And lots of earthquakes. But I wouldn't worry about it," said Rafael.

Chapter 2

The next day Rafael left for Sydney. Three weeks later, Ana and the kids landed in Sydney. Rafael was waiting for them.

"Hey, Dad!" Lilia shouted. Then she ran over to hug her father.

"How was your trip?" Rafael asked. "No, wait. Don't tell me. It was long."

Franco and Antonio rolled their eyes at their father.

"Sorry, but you're not done flying yet," Rafael said. "Tonight we're staying in Sydney. But tomorrow we're off to Port Vila. That's the capital of Vanuatu. Then we'll take another short flight to Tanna. That's the island where we're staying."

"It'll be worth it," Franco said. "As soon as we hit the beach, we'll forget about the planes."

"That's true," said Antonio. "You won't be able to get me out of the water."

Early the next morning, the Silvas flew to Port Vila. There they took a very small plane to Tanna. John Maleki met them at the airport.

He was the owner of the Blue Sea Bungalows. The Silvas were staying there.

They drove past crystal blue waters and sandy beaches. Then they pulled up to the Blue Sea Bungalows. There were tropical plants and trees with colorful birds everywhere. The Silvas looked at the huts where they would be staying. It was paradise.

"Wow!" Franco exclaimed. "This place is awesome."

"Tanna is one of those rare places that isn't spoiled. For the next week we can just enjoy nature. There's no TV, Internet, or fast food" said Rafael. "But there's lots of fishing and diving. And this beautiful beach to enjoy."

"Mr. Maleki said that Tanna is great for snorkeling," Lilia said. "Dad, we're going to unpack and change into our bathing suits. Is it okay if Antonio and I go for a swim?"

"Sure Lilia," Rafael replied. "But stay together."

Chapter 3

Lilia and Antonio put their towels,
sunscreen, and snorkeling gear
in a bag. Then they headed to
the beach. The sand was soft and
white. The water was very blue. No
one else was there. There were huts
sitting over the water. Small boats
rested on the sand. They could see
a mountain. It was the volcano that
Rafael had talked about. They put

down their bag and ran into the water.

They swam out in the clear, warm water. And rode the waves to the shore.

Antonio got his snorkeling gear. Lilia was right behind him.

Out on the reef, they saw a lot of fish and sea creatures.

"Look at that smooth, dark rock," Antonio said. "I think that's lava. There must have been a big eruption here."

After exploring for an hour, they swam back to shore.

Rafael and Franco were on the beach. "How's the water?" Franco asked.

"It's great," Lilia said. "The water's really warm. And it's so clear you can see everything."

"There's a reef out there," Antonio said. "Come out with me, Franco. Let's dive for shells."

"How deep is the water around the reef?" Franco asked.

"It's about fifteen feet. We don't need our air tanks," Antonio answered.

"Hold on, guys," Rafael said. "There's something you have to be careful about in the South Pacific."

"What, Dad?" Antonio asked.

"Moray eels," Rafael replied. "They live in the reef. They wait for something tasty to swim by. Moray eels can grow up to four feet long. And they are very strong and dangerous. So don't stick your hands into any holes in the reef."

"Moray eels, huh? Have you ever seen one?" Franco asked.

"Yes, when I dove in Hawaii for the navy," Rafael said. "I'll never forget it. We were working on a reef close to shore. There were a lot of waves that day. The current was strong. It was hard to stay in one spot.

"One of our divers grabbed some coral so he wouldn't float away," Rafael continued. "He had no idea there was a huge moray eel living in it. When the diver came out of the water, his hand was bleeding. He looked down and two of his fingers were gone!"

"Are you kidding?" Antonio gasped.

"Nope. His fingers were bitten off. Like I told you, eels are strong and dangerous," said Rafael. "But if you don't bother them, they won't bother you."

Rafael and Lilia took a walk along the beach. The boys went in the water.

"I won't be sticking my hands in any holes. I don't care if I see gold coins down there!" Antonio exclaimed.

Twenty minutes later Antonio's pockets were filled with shells. But he wanted more. So he dove down deeper. Then Antonio saw something thin and dark in the coral. Alone and scared, he surfaced and swam over to Franco.

"I think I just saw an eel," Antonio said.

"No way! Where?" Franco asked.

"Over there," Antonio replied. "Follow me."

Franco swam behind Antonio.

"I could only see part of it. So I'm not sure how big it is," Antonio said. "Look below us."

Franco dove below the surface. A moray eel stared up at him. The eel's mouth was open. Franco could see its rows of sharp teeth. Franco remembered his dad's story. He shivered thinking about those razor-sharp teeth biting him. And he quickly swam to the top.

"Yep, that's a moray eel. Let's get out of here!" Franco exclaimed. "I'm going back to the bungalows."

Chapter 4

"Hey, Lilia!" Antonio called out. "Let's take a walk up the beach."

For fifteen minutes they walked without talking. After all the traveling and swimming, it was nice to enjoy the quiet.

Before long they saw a few small huts. People in native clothes were cooking by the water.

"Hello there! Make sure you don't get lost," a voice called out.

Antonio and Lilia turned around. They saw an old man sitting on a boat. He was fixing a fishing net and smoking a pipe.

"Hi," Lilia said. "We won't get lost. We're staying up the beach at the Blue Sea Bungalows."

"Ah," the man answered. "I thought so. You've walked a long way. But you'll be able to get back before dark. No problem."

"Is that your fishing net?" Antonio asked. "We saw a lot of fish on the reef today. The colors were amazing."

"Oh yes. We have many beautiful fishes here," the man replied.

Lilia and Antonio introduced themselves. He said that his name was Simon Mantou. He was a fisherman.

"You are American, right?" Simon asked. "I am 'ni-Tannese.' I've lived on Tanna my whole life. I was a little boy when American soldiers were here. They taught me English."

"Your island is beautiful and peaceful," Lilia said.

"Yes, Tanna is a very peaceful place. Well, it's peaceful most of the time," Simon replied.

"What do you mean by most of the time?" Antonio asked.

"Well, when I was young, the sea turned very ugly one day. In fact, it went wild. There was a tsunami," Simon said.

"I know about tsunamis," Antonio said. "I learned about them in school. A tsunami is a huge tidal wave. I can't believe you saw one!"

Simon put his pipe down. He looked at Antonio.

"When I was eight years old," Simon began. "I was fishing with my father. We were two miles from the shore. I remember the boat rising as a very big wave passed below us."

"Did it do any damage?" Lilia asked.

"No, not then. It didn't become dangerous until it reached shore.

Out in the water, the wave passed under us. But my father knew something was wrong," Simon said.

"What did he do?" Antonio asked.

"I remember it so well. He was staring back toward the island. But Tanna wasn't there! All we could see was a huge wall of water. The island had disappeared. Except for our sacred mountain."

Lilia's eyes were wide. "Then what happened?" she asked.

"My father said to me, 'Simon, we must get back! Something terrible is happening.' It took us two hours to row back to the island," Simon said. "All that time my father was praying."

"What happened when you reached the island?" Antonio asked.

"Oh, it was terrible!" Simon went on. "It was the most horrible thing I have ever seen. Everything was gone! Houses, trees, animals, even people had been washed into the sea.

Remember the wave I said passed under us in deep water? It had turned into a fifty-foot wall of death and destruction."

"That's so awful!" Lilia cried.

"Yes, it was. The sea was calm again, so my father pulled our boat onto the beach. He was looking around. Tears were running down his cheeks. Soon I was crying too," Simon said.

"Our home was gone. Everything was buried in the sand. There wasn't much left of our beautiful island," Simon said. "And what was left was a big mess. But it could have been worse."

"How could it have been worse?" Antonio asked.

"Because the mountain saved many of my people," Simon replied.

"I don't understand. What do you mean?" Antonio asked.

"Well, every year my people pick fruit on the mountain. That year's harvest came two weeks early. Most of the people were gathering fruit. They weren't in the lowlands near the shore," Simon continued. "So they were saved."

"Wow!" Lilia exclaimed. "They sure were lucky."

"No, it was not luck! The sacred mountain protected us," said Simon. "That's why it gave us fruit two weeks early. The mountain knew there was an earthquake nearby. It knew a tsunami was coming. The mountain wanted my people on high ground. It saved us. That is why we get upset when outsiders hurt our mountain."

Chapter 5

The sun was setting. Lilia and
Antonio knew it was time to leave.
They said good-bye to Simon Mantou.

But before leaving, Antonio asked
Simon if there could ever be another
tsunami. "Maybe," said the old man.
"But that is not the greatest danger
to Tanna now."

"What could be more dangerous?"
Antonio asked.

Simon pointed toward the mountain. "That is," Simon said.

The pair walked back to the Blue Sea Bungalows. Later that night Antonio and Lilia told their family about Simon Mantou.

"Can you believe it?" Antonio said. "He survived a tsunami!"

"I think I read about that tsunami," Franco said. "There was a bad one about seventy years ago. It wiped out a lot of the small South Pacific Islands."

"I think you're right," Rafael added. "If Simon saw that one, he would be about eighty years old. Does that sound right?"

"Yeah," Lilia said.

"I think that big tsunami was caused by an earthquake. The quake happened on another island far away," Franco said.

"That's right!" Antonio exclaimed. "Tsunamis come from earthquakes and volcanic eruptions. They can travel thousands of miles."

Lilia liked that Simon believed the mountain had saved his people. "Why do you think he feels that way?" she asked.

"The people on Tanna believe that the mountain is magical," said Rafael. "It's strange to us. But these islanders live a very different life than we do. They have a very close connection with nature."

"That's true," Ana added. "These islanders live a lot like their ancestors. They spend every day of their lives on this little island. They've heard many stories about how powerful their mountain is."

"Do you mean the power the volcano has to erupt?" Lilia asked.

"Yes," Ana replied. "Just imagine what a devastating event that would be!"

"Yeah, it would be horrible," Lilia agreed.

"But an eruption leaves more than death and destruction behind," Ana continued. "It leaves life. Ash from an eruption makes farmland fertile. So the mountain gives life and takes it away. That's why the mountain has a strong impact on the people's beliefs.

"John Maleki told me an interesting story. A big logging company came here twenty-five years ago. They came to harvest wood from the mountain. They were here for two weeks when the volcano erupted. It destroyed their camp. Several loggers were killed. The company had to shut down," Ana said.

"Remember, the islanders view the volcano as a sacred place. They believe the mountain speaks to them. They feel the loggers were punished for disturbing it," Rafael reminded them.

"Well, I guess the volcano is happy now," said Lilia. "There's not too much going on here. It can't get mad at tourists."

"Not any more," Rafael said. "A French company just arrived in Tanna. They've been trying to get a permit here for years. They want to turn a section of the mountain into a coffee farm. They got a permit six months ago. They started clearing the site last week."

Antonio looked at his sister. "Now I get it! That's what Simon meant. Don't you remember, Lilia?" Antonio asked. "Simon told us that the mountain itself is the island's greatest danger."

Chapter 6

For the next three days, the Silvas
explored Tanna. Every afternoon
they swam in the warm water.
Rafael and Franco went scuba
diving off the reef. Ana, Lilia, and
Antonio hiked near the mountain.

But the next morning the earth
shook. The Silvas had planned to hike
near the volcano. The shaking woke
up Lilia and Antonio very early.

"What was that?" cried Lilia.

"Whoa, I don't know," said Antonio.

Just then Rafael came into the room. "Hey, kids. Don't worry. I guess the Ring of Fire is acting up. There have been a couple of quakes deep in the ocean," Rafael explained. "We won't hike near the volcano today."

"Well, I'm going outside," said Lilia. "Come on, Antonio. Let's go to the beach."

When they got to the water, Antonio gasped. "Look over there, Lilia. Was all that smoke there yesterday?" Antonio was pointing toward the volcano.

Lilia stared at the volcano too. A long trail of smoke was coming out of the top.

Antonio looked down at his feet. The sand seemed to be moving under him. How strange! It was like something was shaking the ground.

"Let's not go swimming now," Antonio said. "We should try to find Simon."

Lilia and Antonio walked the same way they had their first day on Tanna. Soon they saw a group of islanders standing by the water. A lot of small boats were tied up near them. Antonio saw Simon Mantou

"Hello, Simon!" Antonio called out. "Is something going on? There's smoke coming out of the mountain."

Antonio felt more rumbling under his feet. All the islanders started talking. They sounded upset.

"The mountain is angry," Simon said. "My people think it's because workers are cutting down trees."

Simon looked at the volcano. He looked worried.

"What should we do?" Lilia asked.

"Pray that the mountain will become calm again. Maybe it will be better tomorrow," said Simon.

"What if tomorrow isn't peaceful?" Antonio asked. "What if it gets even angrier?"

"Then we must leave Tanna," Simon answered. "We must find a safer island with higher ground.

Antonio and Lilia said good-bye to Simon. They hurried back to the Blue Sea Bungalows.

Back at the bungalows, Rafael and Ana were talking to John. Franco was on the porch listening.

"There you two are," Rafael said. "Something's happening to the volcano. We're not sure if it's from the earthquakes. But something is going on."

"That's right," said John. "We shouldn't get too close until things calm down. Right now there's smoke and sparks. It wouldn't be safe."

"That's what we came to tell you, Dad," Antonio said. "We saw smoke coming out of the volcano. So we talked to Simon Mantou about it."

"Why did you talk to Simon about the smoke?" asked Ana.

"Well, he's a native," Lilia answered. "So we thought he might know. He says his mountain is upset. Plus with the earthquakes and all, it's dangerous here."

Ana frowned. She looked at the mountain.

"What do you think, John? Should we be worried?" Ana asked.

"I'm on the radio to Port Vila," John answered. "I've asked about tsunami warnings from the quakes. There's never been an eruption and a tsunami at the same time," he said. "For now, we should stay put."

"The volcano erupted before when loggers cut down trees. Just like they're doing now!" exclaimed Lilia. "It has nothing to do with earthquakes."

Chapter 7

Early the next morning, the Silvas woke to a loud bang. The island rumbled. Was that an aftershock or the volcano? They ran out of their huts.

"It's the volcano!" Antonio exclaimed.

The other guests at the Blue Sea Bungalows had come out of their huts too. Everyone looked at

the volcano. Another loud bang!
The smoke had gotten worse. Now
red-hot sparks flew into the sky.
Huge rocks shot out of the top and
tumbled down the mountain. Each
bang made the earth shake.

John Maleki came speeding down
the beach in his jeep.

"Everyone, please listen up,"
John said. "It looks like we're in
for a big eruption. There's also a
tsunami warning. It's too dangerous
here. We must hurry to the island's
south end."

Antonio stared at the volcano. A
river of hot lava ran down the side.
Everything it touched burst into
flames. A large cloud of ash was

forming over the mountaintop. It was so dark that it blocked the sun.

Then Antonio scanned the sea looking for high waves. But it looked calm. Would a tsunami wash out the island forever? Or would they be buried beneath hot lava?

"It's too late to get off the island by plane," said John. "Our tiny airstrip is at the base of the mountain. It's buried under rocks. The only way off the island is by boat. But there aren't enough boats to hold all of us."

The tourists started to panic.

"Will we be safe on the south end? What about the tsunami?" a man asked.

"I don't know," John answered. "But it will be much safer than here."

The Silvas gathered their things. Because the roads were damaged, everyone started walking down the beach. They all scanned the ocean for the huge wave.

The loggers working on the mountain were panicked. Hot ash rained down on their camp. It was hard for them to breathe with all the ash in the air. Several fires had broken out. But the biggest danger was the lava. The logging camp was in its path.

Some of the loggers were lucky. They'd piled into a working truck. But most of them were running on foot. Slipping and falling, they headed south too. Not all of them would make it.

On the beach, Simon Mantou and the other fishermen watched the eruption.

"It's just as we feared," Simon said. "The mountain is angry about being disturbed. After the loggers are gone, it will calm down. And if the tsunami hits, we will rebuild again."

The fishermen knew it was time to go. They pushed their boats into the water. After a last look at their huts, they rowed south.

Chapter 8

The southern tip of Tanna was very windy. It had rocky beaches. The waves pounded the shore.

Every minute the eruption became more violent. Hot sparks fell and small rocks pelted the people. The ash cloud moved south with the wind. Everyone had trouble breathing.

By now the authorities in Port Vila were working on a plan to help.

"Everyone has moved to the south end of the island. What can we do? There's nowhere for a ship to dock," the mayor of Port Vila said.

"We can send a ship to anchor offshore. People can be rowed out to it," the harbor master said.

"Where do we stand on the tsunami?" asked the mayor.

"It's coming. But we have time. And it's losing some strength," said the harbor master.

After talking it over, everyone agreed. The best way to help was to send a boat to the south end of the island.

A ship from the Royal Australian Navy was docked in the harbor at Port Vila. The *Darwin* could make the eighty-mile trip to Tanna in less than three hours. It would just beat the tsunami.

The Silvas finally reached the south end of the island. Huge rocks lined the coast. It was very hard to walk. People slipped and fell. This part of Tanna was rugged. Everyone hoped they wouldn't be here long. At least the villagers had also made it here in their boats.

Chapter 9

The *Darwin* was a very fast ship.
Captain Walker looked over some
charts. It would be hard to get close
to Tanna. The closest he could bring
his ship was half a mile off the
south shore.

Back on the island John Maleki
listened to his radio. He smiled and
jumped up.

"I have good news! We're being rescued," John said. "A ship is on its way from Port Vila. The captain will come as close as he can. But we'll have to get out to the ship ourselves."

"We can take people to the ship," Simon Mantou said. "We have six boats. But we'll need help guiding them through the water. Then we can row out to the ship. Are there any good swimmers here?"

"My sons and I are good swimmers. We can help guide the boats," Rafael said.

"Great! Each boat can hold five people," said Simon. "We'll have to move as fast as possible."

Chapter 10

The *Darwin* finally anchored off of Tanna. The water was rough. The fishing boats were very small and old. They had to make it past the breaking waves without flipping over.

Simon made the first trip with his own family. Rafael and Franco guided the boat. Timing was important. The boat had to get over the top of a wave. If the wave broke first, the boat would tip over.

Rafael and Franco had to make sure the boat headed straight into the wave. Simon's boat made it over. The crowd cheered.

Four hours later, the last group of passengers was ready to go.

"Wow, what was *that*?" Ana gasped. She felt the ground shake. "Let's hurry."

Ana, Antonio, and Lilia were in the boat. Rafael and Franco guided it out and then jumped in.

Everyone who made it to the south shore was finally on the *Darwin*. They all watched in awe as a giant wave swept over the south end of the island. The island disappeared except for the erupting volcano.

The ship headed back to Port Vila. Simon put his arms around Lilia and Antonio. The old fisherman looked sad.

"Don't worry," Lilia said. "You'll be back home soon."

"I'll be back," said Simon. "But it won't be soon. It will be a long time until the island is well."

"At least everyone will believe you now," said Antonio. "The eruption proves that people should leave the mountain alone. And the tsunami proves how angry the mountain was."

"Hmm. In another twenty or thirty years from now some other

company will come along," said Simon. "They'll cut down trees too. But I won't be around to see it."

That night the Silvas had dinner in Port Vila.

"Well, Rafael," Ana said. "You did it again."

"What did I do this time?" asked Rafael.

"You took us on another trip that almost killed us!" Ana exclaimed.

"Come on," Rafael replied. "You can't blame me for a volcanic eruption *and* a tsunami! It was just really bad luck."

"I guess not," said Ana. "But you have to admit, you are a jinx!"